# All AT SEA

## A collection of Sea Stories

Annie Holland

John Holland

All At Sea
Copyright © 2017 Eggshell Editions

www.stellathestork.com

I would like to acknowledge gratefully Gill McEvoy's editorial skills together with Bev Cowperthwaite technical help, Dee Foy's artistic contribution and Joe Mallon for his help and encouragement.

For all my friends in Portugal who
shared those golden years.

The tale behind the tales….

These stories were written and illustrated by John Holland and myself to entertain children who, like us, in the 1970's/80's were living aboard boats for long periods of time. It also proved to be very entertaining as we had great fun working on them.

The technical age in Portugal was in its infancy and pleasures simple. There was a scarcity of reading material and much exchanging of books amongst the boating community.

Our boat ALMA was moored, at Quatros Aguas (where Doris the Dredger still lives) in Tavira on the Algarve.

The weekly barbeques were eagerly looked forward to when the 'boaties' gathered to exchange news, socialise and listen to the latest adventures of Captain Cuttle.

Sadly, only four of these stories remain as the rest were lost when the boat capsized. A dramatic sinking would have made a good story – however, it was more mundane, someone left a bung open, the water entered and reached the lockers where the stories and drawings were stowed. The eagle-eyed amongst you may spot some water damage and restoration on some of the pictures. Longer journeys often resorted in running out of writing materials and resorting to using scrappy pieces of paper and odd crayons! Hence some of the discrepancies in colouration of pictures.

John Holland was well known in the Algarve for his sea and futuristic pictures and held many exhibitions.

Annie Holland.

# Little Red Clock

Whilst walking round the harbour
with time to look and stop
Captain Cuttle saw a bright red clock
in the window of a shop.

For hands it had two sails,
for numbers it had buoys.

"Well, fancy that!" the Captain said,
"A handy little toy."

He went into the clock shop.
The bell went ding-a-ling.
"Good morning!" said the owner,
"Can I help with anything?"

"I'd like to buy that bright red clock
if that's all right with you
it will come in mighty handy
for waking up the crew."

The owner hesitated -
"Are you sure you want to buy?
Agreed, it's very charming
but I'd better clarify -
you simply can't rely on it
it's nothing like Big Ben
it might go off at seven
or maybe not till ten!"

The Captain pondered for a while
then said, "Here's what I'll do -
I'll take the clock back home with me
aboard the Molly Sue.

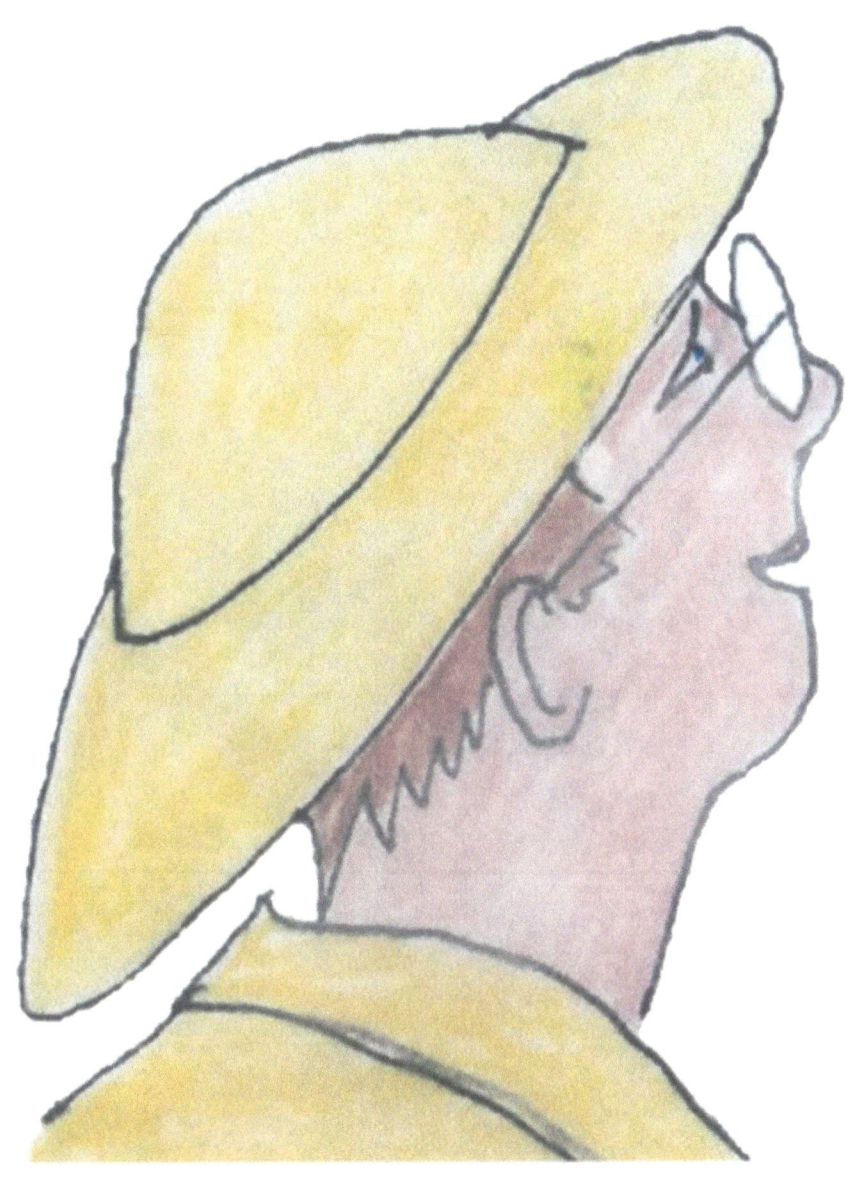

My deckhand, name of Oilskin,
there's nothing he can't do
and if he gets it working well
I'll buy the clock from you."

They both shook hands,
the deal was struck -
all might turn out fine

if Oilskin got it working
so the bell would ring on time.

Oilskin took the clock to bits.
It was quite a work of art!
With cogs and springs and levers
he didn't know where to start.

Then the Captain called,
"Avast there,"
to Oilskin down below,
"Come up here and get to work
for it's off to sea we go!"

Poor Oilskin had to leave the clock
and get himself on deck.
(When you prepare a boat for sea
there's such a lot to check!)

He ran up quickly to the ropes
and cast off all the lines.
He lifted all the fenders in and
they cleared the quay just fine.

Beyond the harbour wind sprung up,
the Molly Sue heeled to it.
They couldn't keep her stable -
there was no way to do it.

But the sea was very choppy
(the passengers turned white)
the clock or duties on the deck
he'd never felt in such a plight.

The journey did not last too long
the passengers were sick.
They begged the Captain, "Come about,
return to port real quick!"

When the boat was back in port
and everything was calm,
Oilskin went to work again
to fix the clock's alarm.
He worked for many hours
to repair the little clock,
and when he got it all together,
it made a loud 'tick-tock'.

He did not try the clock's alarm,
no time to check it out,
for from the deck he heard again
The Captain's booming shout
"Avast there, Mr Oilskin,
we're off to sea again,
so leave that clock and get up here
and don't you dare complain."

They set off for some islands.
the boat went fast and slick.

Dee Foy

But as they neared the island rocks
a fog fell, grey and thick.
No one could see further
than the foresail from the deck.
So they had to drop the anchor
before the ship got wrecked.

As they lay there safe at anchor
the crew all went below
while Oilskin stayed upon deck
to watch for the fog to go.
But Oilskin was tired
he soon began to snore
and as he slept the anchor lost
its grip on the ocean floor.

A current caught the Molly Sue
and pushed her close to rocks.

Before she hit, the bell rang out
from the newly-mended clock.

"Quick, Oilskin, start the engine,
shake off that sleepy pose.
When you're on the anchor watch
you're not supposed to doze!"

"Hoorah" cried Captain Cuttle
as he turned the ship around."
If it were not for that little red clock
we'd have surely run aground."

When the Molly Sue returned to port
and was safely in the dock,
Captain Cuttle told the story
of the little mended clock.

"That clock," he said, "has saved the
day by sounding its alarm.
It rang so loud – it woke us up
and saved us all from harm."

The Captain went back to the shop
to settle the account -
(he would have been prepared to pay
a VERY HUGE amount.)

The clock-man was so happy
that no one had been drowned.
he let the Captain have the clock
for just a single pound!

# Best Mates!

Captain Cuttle, Oilskin
and Jinx the ship's cat.

The End©

Cover Dee Foy

On a lovely summer morning
in the Port of Pollywash
when the boats were a-bobbing on the tide
with happy splish and splosh.

There moored beside the jetty
was a boat named Polly Sue.
A boat that had no sails
but was driven by a screw.

The engine of the Polly Sue
that day refused to start
so Captain Cuttle was below
straightening out her parts.

He heard a voice call out to him
"Ahoy! Is this boat to rent?"
And when the Captain came aloft
he saw a fine young gent.

"Come on board Sir," said the Captain,
"I've nearly got her started.
We'll catch the tide and off we'll go
all ship-shape, hale and hearty."
The sea was rougher than he thought,
and the passenger felt ill.

The Captain looked at him and said,
"Young man, you're green about the gills!"
But soon the sea became quite calm,
and they got the rods and bait
then cast their fishing lines outboard
and settled down to wait.

But not a bite for hours on end -
"We might as well go back."
But as the boat was turned for home
there came a mighty crack....

The line astern stretched taut and firm,
"Good grief! We've caught a shark,"
cried Charles, the elegant young gent,
"Oh, what a jolly lark."
But not as jolly as it seemed
the Polly Sue stopped dead.
The thing they'd caught was stopping
her from moving off ahead.

Young Charles was very worried
and he ran to cut the line -
"Wait," cried the Captain,
"The fish will tire,
we'll bring it in just fine.

And if we've caught a fish that big
I might just settle down.
There's a little place I fancy
in the swanky part of town."

The fish must be enormous
on this they both agreed
for it was pulling them
far, far away to sea.
At last the pace slackened
the strain came off the gear.
The Captain started hauling in
but not without some fear.

A SHAPE LEAPT FROM THE WATER!
"Good grief a periscope!
If there's a fish attached to that
we're going to need some rope."

When the 'fish' came into view
it made them start to scream.
They hadn't caught a fish at all
but a great big....

# S U B M A R I N E !

The End©

# DAPHNE THE DINGHY

DAPHNE the Dinghy lay upside down
in a tangle of pots and weeds
and she was really most unhappy
being so far from the sea.

One day a jolly sailor,
Captain Cuttle was his name,
spotted poor old Daphne,
as he sauntered down the lane.
"Avast! What have we here then?"
he uttered with great glee,
"I've been looking for a dinghy,
this one will do for me."

He rat-a-tatted on the door
Daphne's owner soon appeared.
"Good morning," said the Captain
with his happy salty cheer,
"I'd like to buy that dingy
If that's all right with you.
I need another tender -
it will come in useful for my crew."

The lady said, "Dear Captain,
please take it with my blessing,
it's nothing but a nuisance here,
it makes the place look messy."

The Captain brought his trailer.
Daphne soon was stowed.
He and the dinghy (right side up)
went swiftly down the road.

He went to buy some paint
and left Daphne on the quay.
She felt so very happy
to be so near the sea.

Whilst he was gone a small boy tripped
and fell into the sea.

And the lifebuoy – it was stolen,
the young lad could not swim!

Some people grabbed the dinghy

and quickly launched her in.

Daphne brought the boy to shore,
His frightened face was grey.

Those who'd watched the rescue roared,
"Hip hip! Hip hip! Hooray!"

Captain Cuttle soon returned
and got a full report.
How proud he felt
to own a dinghy of this sort.

Daphne was soon painted
and everyone agreed
that she looked quite ecstatic
to be back upon the sea.

# A MESSAGE
## FROM CAPTAIN CUTTLE

Never steal a lifebuoy
that is hanging by the quay
for it could save your life,
if you should fall into the sea.

The End©

# DORIS the DREDGER

## and

# The Big Storm

DORIS THE DREDGER lived in the far corner of a big harbour.

It was so lonely and Doris often felt very sad.

The only person who ever had a kind word for her was the Harbour Master and a passing seagull.

There was an entrance to the harbour between two long stone walls called breakwaters. This entrance always had to be kept clear.

On each breakwater sat a small lighthouse with a flashing light.
The portside light (on the left) was red and the starboard light (on the right) was green.

These lights guided the boats safely from the sea into the harbour.

Every day Doris the Dredger worked in the harbour entrance.

Using her bucket and crane, she would dig a channel removing all the sand that had been brought in by the night tide. Time and time again Doris had to load it onto her deck and carry it back to the dockside. It was very tiring.

When Doris was fully loaded, she sank so low in the water that she looked like a submarine.
Because she had such a dirty job Doris was always wet and rusty. Very few people even knew she had a name.

All the other boats, brightly painted and flying their flags were great friends and had a happy time playing together.

Competitions and races would be held and when they came back from sea they would all go to the Yacht Club and have a party, except for Doris who was never invited.

Doris was big and slow.

When working, she got in the way of the other boats who thought she was a great nuisance.

They waved their fists and shouted at her. In fact, they were very rude.

This made poor Doris so unhappy as she wanted to be friends with everyone.

Whenever the weather was fine, the fishing boats with nets, coloured balls and floats on their decks would head out to sea.

On their return people would crowd onto the dock to buy the fresh silver, glistening fish.

One weekend, there was a big regatta and the boats came from all over to take part. Even the fishing boats were invited. As usual Doris was ignored.

When the boats were out racing a large wave knocked down the sides of the entrance channel and it quickly filled with sand.

When they returned they couldn't get back in!

To make matters worse, the Harbour Master then came on the radio and told them that a big storm was heading towards them.

The boats all knew that they were in great danger and began to feel frightened. They asked the Harbour Master for help.

"Our only hope now is Doris the Dredger," he told them.

The wind was howling and the sky was getting blacker as the Harbour Master rushed over to where Doris was resting.

"The channel has filled up and all the boats are trapped out at sea. There is a big storm coming. We need you. Can you...will you help us PLEASE Doris?" he begged.

Doris opened a weary eye and for a second hesitated as she remembered how unpleasant everyone had been to her – well you couldn't blame her could you?

But her good nature got the better of her and she said, "Yes, of course, I will do my very best."

As the Harbour Master untied her mooring Doris took a deep breath and then went full speed to the harbour entrance to set to work.

Doris scooped the sand out so quickly that she thought the nuts and bolts from her crane would come loose. When she was full, the dredger went at top speed back into the harbour to unload the sand. She made the journey seven times, there and back, before the channel was clear. Doris had never worked so fast or so hard.

Doris managed to clear the harbour entrance in record time.

The Harbour Master radioed all the boats and told them it was now safe.

A great cheer went up and everyone hooted and tooted at Doris as they returned home.

"Hooray! Hooray! Doris has saved the day", they all chanted as they blew their horns, dipped their sails and cheered as the last boat managed to get to safety. The big storm lasted a long time and there was a lot of damage but thanks to Doris all the boats in the harbour were safe.

When the storm had blown itself out, the yachts and fishing boats asked the Harbour Master to apologise to Doris for their bad behaviour and to thank her for saving them.

As for the Harbour Master, he was so pleased with Doris that he gave her a month off work so that she could rest and have some repairs as her nuts and bolts were aching and she was starting to rattle.

Then, as a special reward, he had her painted bright blue, put coloured flags on her mast and best of all, her name 'DORIS' was written in big letters on both her sides. Doris the Dredger was beside herself with happiness.

There was a lot of damage that night of the big storm and many boats out at sea sank.

It took the big storm to make everyone realise what a very valuable and special boat Doris was.

How different it all is now, for every-one wants to be friends with Doris and she has so many visitors.

A special regatta is held every year on the anniversary of the big storm.

DORIS THE DREDGER DAY is the highlight of the year.

All the boats compete to win the DORIS CUP which Doris the Dredger always presents to the winner.

The End©

Annie Holland

Author of Stella the Stork children's stories, writer, journalist, event organiser, blog writer

*John Holland*
*1937 – 2000*
*Sailor, actor, writer, artist*
*and conservationist*

This book is also available on Kindle and Audio narrated by Patrick Montello

Patrick Montello is a voice actor who grew up in Hull, Massachusetts. He has been involved in theatre since the 1980's and spent about 10 years in morning radio, producing, writing and performing comedy for various radio stations. He has sold many comedy bits to 'The Olympia Network', a service that provides comedy to radio stations in the USA. He loves history, cooking, language and has a BA in Anthropology. His sole desire in life is to own a sailboat and a monkey and sail to the Tortugas as soon as he can find out where that is!

www.ingramcontent.com/pod-product-compliance
Lightning Source LLC
Chambersburg PA
CBHW041408010726
47507CB00001B/44